ELMHURST PUBLIC LIBRARY
3 1135 00780 26
W9-AST-380

THE NANCY DREW NOTEBOOKS®

#49

The Sand Castle Mystery

CAROLYN KEENE
ILLUSTRATED BY PAUL CASALE

Aladdin Paperbacks
New York London Toronto Sydney Singapore

First Aladdin Paperbacks edition August 2002

ALADDIN PAPERBACKS
An imprint of Simon & Schuster
Children's Publishing Division
1230 Avenue of the Americas
New York, NY 10020

The text of this book was set in Excelsior.

Printed in the United States of America
10 9 8 7 6 5

Library of Congress Control Number 2001097939

ISBN 0-7434-3767-5

1

The Greatest Sand Castle Contest Ever

"What this sand castle needs is a seashell!" eight-year-old Nancy Drew exclaimed to her best friends, Bess Marvin and George Fayne.

Nancy gently pressed a pale pink shell along the bottom of their castle. So far, their castle was still pretty small, and it had only one tower, but Nancy still liked it. "Do you think we have a chance at winning the sand castle contest?" Nancy asked.

"I know we do!" Bess said, giving George a high five.

George and Bess were cousins. George's real name was Georgia but she liked to be called George. All three girls went to the same school and now that it was summer they were on a special four-day vacation together. Carson Drew, Nancy's father, was a lawyer, and he had taken the girls with him on a business trip. He had rented a cottage at the edge of Echo Lake in Michigan. Nancy thought it was the most beautiful lake in the whole world.

Hannah Gruen, Nancy's housekeeper, had come along, too. Hannah had taken care of Nancy for the past five years, ever since her mom passed away. She always made sure Nancy had clean clothes and ate balanced meals. Now at Echo Lake she could watch the girls at the beach from the kitchen window of the cottage.

Ever since the girls had arrived at the beach on Friday, all they could think or talk about was Echo Lake's Tenth Annual Sand Castle Building Contest.

Bright yellow fliers about it were posted all over town. Anyone between the ages of six and twelve could enter, and Nancy, George, and Bess had signed up right away. It was Saturday now, and the girls had until Monday afternoon to make the best, most beautiful sand castle they could imagine.

"I can taste the first prize," Bess said. She licked her lips. "All the ice cream you can eat after the contest at Peppermint Park!"

"Did you see those flavors on the flier?" Nancy said. "Mmmm, Beachy Peachy Fudge."

"S'mores Scores," George said.

"You would pick the flavor that had to do with sports." Nancy laughed.

"The winners get their pictures in the newspaper, too. Plus your picture will hang in Peppermint Park for a year!" said Bess. She picked up her baseball cap and yanked it onto her head. "Maybe I'll wear my new hat for the photo!" Bess laughed. She tugged the brim down over her blue eyes and made a silly face.

"I'm going to bring the picture home and show Brenda," said George. Brenda Carlton went to their school and always bragged about the newspaper she ran. "I bet the *Echo Lake News* is better than her old paper, any day," George said.

"We haven't won yet," Nancy said. She looked around the special roped-off area of the beach. In every corner were groups of people working on castles. Nancy did a quick count. "We have ten other teams we have to beat," she said. They were team number nine, and there was a red flag with the number on it right by their castle.

Bess opened her beach bag and took out two drawings of sand castles.

"It's a good thing the contest didn't start until today," Bess said. "I'm glad we had time to go to the library and study up on castles."

George wriggled her fingers. "Yeah, but my fingers are so tired from taking all those notes! I never thought I'd be studying anything on vacation—even something as cool as sand castles."

"Drawing pictures of a castle is one thing," Bess said doubtfully. "Building it is another."

"Some of these castles are amazing," Nancy said as she looked around. There was a castle next to them that had three tall, pointed towers. There was another castle decorated with real starfish.

George looked down at one of the drawings. "Our castle doesn't look like the drawings we did," she said. "I wanted it to have two, maybe even three big towers, and lots and lots of windows."

"Our castle still looks like a big lump," Bess said.

"It does not. We have to think positively," Nancy said. "And I positively think we are going to win."

Nancy dug in her beach bag and pulled out a straw. "I read about this in one of the books. This is for blowing away extra sand," she said. She leaned over the castle and gently blew into the straw.

Bess took water from a pail and poured a little on some sand. "This will help the sand pack down tightly," she said. Then she put the wet sand in one of Hannah's cooking molds. It was the shape of a small fish.

"Here goes nothing!" Bess said, and carefully turned the mold over on top of one of the towers. When she lifted it up, there was the shape of a fish.

"That looks great," George said. "But I think we need something more to give it oomph."

Bess frowned. "But what?"

"Let's take a picture of it," Nancy said.

"Maybe we can figure something out tonight."

Nancy pulled out three bright yellow disposable cameras and held them up. The best thing about them was that they were waterproof and Nancy could take pictures under the water if she wanted. Nancy's father had bought them the cameras because he hadn't wanted to miss any of the fun while he was working. "Pictures will be the next best thing to being there," he said.

The girls loved the cameras. Already they had taken pictures of the cottage, inside and out. They had even taken pictures of their own feet walking on the sandy bottom of the lake.

Nancy snapped a picture of the castle. "Come on, let's take pictures of all the other castles, too," she said.

Bess grabbed her camera and snapped a picture of the team next to them. Then Nancy took a picture of the lifeguard and the team nearest to him. He was sitting high up on a white chair. He had a stripe of white sunblock on his nose, which made her laugh.

Sandcastle
Design

"Say ice cream!" Nancy said, taking a picture of Bess.

"Hot fudge!" Bess laughed.

The girls took the cameras down to the water and dove under the surface with them. Nancy opened her eyes wide and took a picture of Bess. Then Bess took a picture of George. All three girls sputtered and came up for air.

"Hey, cool camera! Is it waterproof?" asked a voice. Nancy turned. The two girls from the sand castle next to them were in the water, too. They both had on the same blue bathing suit. "Can I see the camera?" one girl asked, and Nancy handed it to her.

"Major cool," the girl said. She handed the camera back to Nancy, smiling.

"I'll take your picture, too," Nancy said, "but first tell me your names so I'll know whose pictures I'm taking."

"I'm Lara," said the girl with the long brown braids. "I'm Jane," said her friend, who had short, curly brown hair.

Nancy took their picture. "Got you!" she said. "Your castle is really awesome. How did you get the tops to point up like that?"

"That might just be the *winning* secret," said Lara, smiling.

"We won second prize last year, but this year we're going to win first!" said Jane.

"No, *we* are," giggled Bess.

Jane smiled back at Bess. "We've been building sand castles here every summer since the contest started. This is our year to win."

"Did you just move here?" Lara asked Nancy. "Where do you live?"

George shook her head. "I wish we lived here! We're on vacation."

Lara's face grew dark. "That's not fair! This contest should be for the people who live here, not people like you who are just on vacation."

Get out of My Way!

Nancy was shocked—these girls didn't want Nancy and her friends to enter the contest!

"Now, just wait a minute," a kindly voice said.

Nancy glanced up. An older woman in a pretty blue-flowered summer dress came over. Her hair was soft gray and rippling with curls. Her eyes were as blue as the flowers on her dress.

Next to her, scribbling something in a notebook, was a man wearing a T-shirt and jeans, with a baseball cap low on his head. Around his neck was a badge that said PRESS on it in big blue letters.

He introduced himself. "Kurt Jeffers, *Echo Lake News*. Is there trouble here? Trouble sells newspapers."

Jane pointed angrily at Nancy and her friends. "There's the trouble! They don't even live here, so why should they get to be in the contest? It isn't fair!"

The woman shook her head. "Now calm down, girls," she said. She turned to Nancy and her friends. "I'm Mrs. Thorton," she said. "I've run the contest for ten years and I say that everyone is welcome to enter it."

Lara and Jane frowned. "Fine, but we're *still* going to win," Lara said. Lara and Jane headed back to their castle.

"We're happy to have you in our contest," Mrs. Thorton said, turning back toward Nancy, George, and Bess. "If you need anything, you come to me."

"Thank you very much," Nancy said.

"Yes, thank you," echoed Bess and George.

Mrs. Thorton touched Kurt Jeffers's arm. "We'd better be going," she said.

"That's right," Kurt Jeffers said. "The news waits for no man!"

"Or woman." Mrs. Thorton laughed. "See you later, girls."

The girls went back to work. Bess took out her plastic library card.

"Bess, this is no time to go to the library! We have enough books about sand castles," George said, but Bess shook her head.

"Watch," Bess said. "I learned this from one of the books we got out." She used the edge of the card to make a swirl design.

"Awesome! If we can find a tiny gardening hoe, we can rake a path around the castle," George said.

"Look," said Nancy, "that team over there is using Popsicle sticks to make a fence. That's a good idea."

"It's not just good, it's great!" said a girl, coming toward them.

"Hi," said Nancy.

"Hi!" said the girl. She had a merry smile and black hair in a pixie cut. "I'm Lisa. Are you new here?" she asked.

"Why? Are you going to tell us to leave?" Bess asked suspiciously. Lisa laughed.

"Leave? Why would I tell you to do that?" She looked at their castle. "What this needs is colored sand," she said.

"Colored sand?" asked Bess. "You mean we should paint it?"

Lisa giggled. "You should *buy* it! The Beach Barn has lots of great sand. I can take you over there later, if you want. It's really close. You can see it from the beach."

"Are you in the contest, too?" George asked.

"I wish," Lisa said sadly. "I won the contest last year, but the rules say you can't win more than once."

She brightened. "But I can help you guys! It will be almost like I am entering again."

Bess brushed sand off her legs. "We could use all the help we can get," she said. "That would be great. Thank you."

Lisa taught the girls lots of cool castle-building tricks. She showed them how an ice cream scoop could build great windows. She showed them how mixing a little glue in the water made the sand stick better.

The girls worked all afternoon and then decided to take a break. "Let me take your picture," Nancy said, and Lisa stood up and posed, putting one hand on her hip.

Nancy took two pictures. Suddenly she

felt a squirt of water on her leg. She turned just in time to see the water hit the sand castle, too! "Hey!" Nancy cried, and looked up to see a boy with a water pistol running in the other direction. He had red hair and a lot of freckles.

"That's James," Lisa said. "He lives here all year round, too." She pointed to a house right next door to the cottage where Nancy and the girls were staying. "Don't pay any attention to him," Lisa said. "He was in my second-grade class last year, and he's a Grade A pest!"

George bent and studied the castle. "It's just a little wet," she said, giving it an extra pat.

"We've worked hard enough today," Nancy said. "Let's go ask Hannah if we can walk to the Beach Barn."

The other girls jumped up. "And to Peppermint Park!" George said.

Hannah gave the girls permission because the shops were so close and she could watch them walk there. But better than that, she also gave them some extra money for ice cream and colored sand.

The walk was bright and sunny. "I can't stop taking pictures," George said, taking a photo of a dog wearing a straw hat.

"Me, neither!" said Bess, as she snapped a picture of a shop window filled with kites.

"Wait until my dad sees this!" Nancy exclaimed, snapping a picture of a girl who had a live parrot on her shoulder.

"And wait until you see Peppermint Park. Here we are," Lisa said.

Peppermint Park had pink and white stripes painted on the outside. "Just like a delicious candy cane," Nancy said, touching the outside stripes. Inside, the booths and tables were all pink and white, too. Nancy tilted her nose in the air. "Mmm, chocolate!" She sighed.

The girls sat at a table and a friendly looking woman in a striped apron came over. Beside her was a girl with brown braids, who looked the same age as Nancy and her friends.

"That's the owner, Mrs. Rhodes, and her daughter, Katharine," said Lisa. "She's really nice."

"Hi Lisa," said Mrs. Rhodes. Lisa introduced Nancy, Bess, and George to Mrs. Rhodes and Katharine.

"Welcome to Peppermint Park!" Mrs. Rhodes said. "Katharine, would you set the table and hand out some menus?"

Katharine put down some napkins and four big candy-striped menus.

"I'm just going to get some water from the fountain over there," Lisa said. "I'll be right back."

"I want to get some pictures of this place," said Nancy. She took a shot of the counter with all the gleaming silver faucets. Then she took a picture of Mrs. Rhodes, and then one of Katharine.

"Hey!" Katharine said, blinking. "You should have let me do my hair." She pulled her braids up so they were standing straight up from her head.

The girls laughed. "You sure have a terrific beach here," Nancy told Katharine. "We're having the best visit ever."

"Thanks," said Katharine, setting down some long silver spoons.

"And a terrific sand castle contest!" Bess

PEPPERM
PARK

exclaimed. "We're so excited we got here in time to enter."

Katharine's face darkened and she got very quiet.

"Maybe later we'll see you at the beach," George said.

Katharine shrugged and then suddenly she turned and walked away from them.

"What was that about?" Bess said. "She looked like someone told her she could never have ice cream again!"

"Gee, she really isn't very friendly," Nancy said. "I thought Lisa said she was nice."

"Maybe she's just having a bad day," George suggested.

Just then, Lisa came back. Mrs. Rhodes returned, too, to take their order. The girls scanned the menus. Never had they seen so many flavors or so many funny names—Butter Me Up Butter Pecan, Choco-lightning, Martian Marshmallow.

"I want all of them!" Bess moaned, and Nancy laughed.

"I want A Fan of Banana," George decided.

"Perfectly Peanuty," Bess said.

"Gorilla Vanilla," Nancy said.

"Coconutty," said Lisa.

"Coming right up," Mrs. Rhodes said.

It didn't take long. Mrs. Rhodes arrived with the ice cream in silver bowls. Nancy had never seen anything that looked more delicious.

The ice cream tasted as good as it looked, maybe even better. Nancy was trapped between wanting to take her time so the ice cream would last, and wanting to gulp it down because she couldn't help herself.

"I'm done," said Bess. "If I eat another bite, I'll turn into ice cream."

"I think you've already started." Nancy laughed. "You have ice cream on your nose!" Bess laughed and wiped her nose with her napkin.

"You guys ready?" Lisa said. "Because the Beach Barn is going to be the most awesome place you've ever seen!"

The girls paid for their ice cream and walked outside. "The Beach Barn is right over there." Lisa pointed to the store.

The Beach Barn had one huge front window, filled with brightly colored sand-pails and shovels. "Inside is even better," Lisa promised.

Lisa opened the door. Suddenly, James rushed out, carrying a package of green sand. "Gangway!" he cried. Then he bumped into Nancy so hard, she tumbled to the sidewalk!

3

A Message in the Sand

"Hey!" Nancy called, dusting herself off, but James had kept running and was too far away to hear her. "Boy, that wasn't nice!"

"Where is he going in such a hurry?" Bess asked.

"Probably off to cause more trouble," Lisa said. "Come on, don't pay him any more attention. Let me show you around."

The Beach Barn had everything you could ever want for the beach—and more, Nancy thought. There were beach towels, sand toys, and a row of colored starfish strung across the ceiling with red yarn. There were big bins of beach balls and pinwheels, and all along the walls were tubs of the most beautiful colored sand Nancy had ever seen. "They've got every color in the rainbow!" she exclaimed.

Bess ran her hands through the blue sand. "Look at this pink sand," George said.

Lisa pointed to a jar of sparkly sand. "The judges would love this," she said.

The girls bought the sparkly sand and then walked back to the beach. It was starting to get cloudy and cooler now. There weren't so many people on the beach.

"I hope it doesn't rain," Bess said. "That would ruin the castle."

"It wouldn't dare!" Lisa said.

"Let's get up really early so we can have a fresh start on our castle," Nancy said. "I can't wait to try out the colored sand."

"Me, neither," said Bess.

"Want to come back to the cottage with us?" Nancy asked Lisa. "We can play cards."

Lisa shook her head. "I have to go to the dentist. My dad's coming to pick me up in a little while."

"Thanks for coming with us," Nancy said to Lisa. The girls all waved good-bye.

That night Nancy, Bess, and George pored over the books on sand castles. Nancy got out some drawing paper and crayons and they drew some plans. George scribbled in a tall tower. "If we pack the sand in hard and use a Popsicle stick, we can cut in stairs," Bess said.

The girls worked all evening, stopping only when Mr. Drew came in. "Time for bed," he said.

"Already?" said Nancy.

"You have another big day ahead of sand castle building," he said.

The girls washed and got into bed, but Nancy was restless. "I'm too excited to sleep," she whispered.

"Count sheep," George said, yawning loudly. "Or better yet, count sand castles."

"Okay," said Nancy doubtfully. She shut her eyes and tried to imagine a row of sand castles walking past her. "One sand castle, two sand castles," she counted. Then she yawned, and soon she was sleeping.

In the morning, the girls were up bright and early. They had blueberry pancakes with Mr. Drew. "It's Sunday and I don't have to work, so I'm going to go to the beach later, too," Mr. Drew said. "Maybe I should enter the contest myself since I have this free time today." His eyes twinkled.

"You can't enter the contest, Dad!" Nancy laughed. "Only kids can."

"Well, you can't blame me for trying." Mr. Drew laughed.

After the girls ate, they ran outside to the beach. "I can't wait to try out the sparkly sand!" George said.

"Hey," said Nancy, "there's a crowd around our castle."

"What are they doing there?" asked George. "Did we do that good a job?"

Nancy frowned. They walked closer. "There's Lisa," George said, waving, but Lisa looked upset and didn't wave back. The girls inched closer and Bess suddenly gasped. There in the sand, in big letters, was written STAY AWAY! Even worse, their castle was destroyed!

Bess's hand flew to her mouth. "How will we ever rebuild our castle in time?" she wailed.

STAY
AWAY!

Nancy looked around the crowd. "Who would do such an awful thing?" she asked.

Mrs. Thorton and Kurt the reporter came racing toward them. "Nothing like this has ever happened before," Mrs. Thorton said.

Kurt took out a notebook. Nancy remembered how he had said trouble sold newspapers, and she didn't like the excited way he was writing. What if the things he was writing caused more trouble? "What happened?" he asked.

"We don't know," Bess said. "We just got here."

"This is terrible," Lisa said. "What are you going to do? Are you going to take yourselves out of the contest?"

"We won't let this stop us!" Nancy exclaimed.

"This happened because no one from out of town has ever entered the contest," Jane said.

"Now that's not fair!" Bess said.

"Is too!" Lara said, putting her hands angrily on her hips.

"Girls," said Mrs. Thorton. "I told you before that everyone can enter. Now we take our contest very seriously and we are going to find out who did such a thing and make sure it doesn't happen again. In the meantime, why don't you girls work at rebuilding your castle." She shook her head. "And we can just erase this nasty 'stay away.'"

"Oh, no, it has to stay!" Nancy cried.

"It does?" George asked. "But it's disturbing."

"That's why *we* can't disturb it," Nancy explained. "It's evidence. It might just help us to find out who did this."

"How's it going to do that?" Bess asked.

Nancy chewed on her lower lip. "I don't know yet," she admitted.

"Well, you're the best detective around, so I bet you'll figure it out," George said.

"If you think leaving that sign will help, then we'll leave it," Mrs. Thorton said.

Mrs. Thorton left and the crowd slowly walked away. The girls sat glumly looking at their castle. It was kicked in on one side. The top was lopsided and the moat Bess had started to build was filled in with sand.

"How will we have time to rebuild?" Bess said. "We have just two more days."

"We can rebuild it," Nancy said. "But what happens if someone comes back and kicks it in again?"

"Nancy, you're the detective. Who do you think did this?" George asked.

Nancy looked around the beach. "I don't know, but we're all going to have to be detectives on this one," she said.

Nancy got her special blue detective notebook and pencil out of her backpack. "Suspects," she said. "We need suspects."

"Do we have any?" Lisa asked.

Nancy chewed on the end of her pencil and wrote "Suspects" at the top of the page.

"What about the reporter?" George said. "Remember, he said trouble was good for selling newspapers."

"Reporter," Nancy wrote down.

"How about Jane and Lara?" said Bess. "They don't think we should be in the contest because we don't live here."

Nancy carefully wrote down their names.

"James is always causing trouble. Maybe

it was him," Lisa said, and Nancy wrote his name, too.

Next, Nancy wrote in big block letters "Clues." She looked up. "We know why these suspects may have done it, but we don't have any clues," she said.

Nancy jumped up. "We have to look around." The girls all studied the castle.

"I see something," said Bess. She pointed to a whirly pattern on a footprint. Nancy crouched down, studying the print.

"Let me see," said George. George bent closer and then sighed.

"What? Why did you sigh?" Nancy asked.

George lifted up one of her sandaled feet. "That's the special pattern on the bottom of my new beach shoes," George said.

"I know," said Nancy, "we'll take pictures of the scene of the crime. My father says that is a good way to discover clues." She dug into her beach bag and got out the cameras. Each girl took a few pictures.

Nancy was about to put her camera back in her bag when she noticed something about the sand. She pointed excitedly. "Look at the color of that sand!" she cried.

The girls looked where Nancy was pointing. There was a thin line of green sand.

"That isn't the color we bought!" Nancy exclaimed.

"But it *is* the color James bought!" cried George.

4

James's Secret

"James did have green sand," said Nancy excitedly. "But we have to prove that he was here and that he ruined our castle."

Lisa scanned the beach. "There he is now," she said. She pointed to the water. James's red head bobbed up and he suddenly splashed another boy.

"Cut that out!" the other boy shouted. James splashed him again and then ran out of the water back onto the sand. When he ran past the girls, he stuck out his tongue.

Bess stuck her tongue out, too, but George grabbed her arm. "Don't make him suspicious of us!" George said.

"Let's follow him," Nancy said. "But don't let him see us!"

James had stopped running and was busy putting on his sneakers. The girls walked toward him.

Nancy suddenly froze. "Do you see what I see?" Nancy whispered.

"I see James, our suspect," Bess said.

Nancy shook her head. "Look closer," she whispered. "He has a green stain on the side of his sneaker—just like the green sand we found on our castle!"

James stood and started walking away from the beach.

"It's lucky he lives next door to our cottage. We can stay on our porch and he won't even know we're spying on him," Bess said.

The girls quickly ran to their porch. They saw James rush into his house and then come out carrying a bag of green sand. Then he slowly opened the sand and poured it into a wooden box.

Just then Lisa sneezed. James looked up and his face went red.

"Guilty!" Bess whispered, but Nancy shook her head.

"We still need proof," Nancy said. "My father always tells me you can't accuse people without proof."

"Hey, what are you doing spying on me?" James said, standing up.

"What are you doing with that green sand?" Bess demanded.

James looked puzzled. "I bought this sand for my sister. I'm surprising her with a special sandbox," James explained.

Now it was Nancy's turn to frown. "But we found green sand by our wrecked castle," Nancy told James. "The same green sand that you're using now."

"So what? I might have run by your stupid castle but I sure didn't destroy it!" James said angrily. "I wouldn't do a thing like that! What kind of guy do you think I am?"

"The kind of guy who squirts sand castles with water guns," George said.

James shook his head. "I just wanted to soak *you*, not your dumb castle," he said.

James crouched down again. A flop of red hair fell into his eyes and he pushed it back. "I have to finish this before my little sister comes back from shopping with my mom. Green is her favorite color." He looked at his watch. "She'll be home any moment. Look, it stinks that your stupid castle was destroyed, but I didn't do it," he said. "Now scram so I can finish my work!"

Nancy took out her detective notebook and found the suspects list. She drew a line through James's name, then sighed. If James didn't do it, then who did?

"Let's go back to the beach and work," she said glumly to her friends. "Maybe we can find some more clues."

The girls walked down to the beach. They looked around, but all they saw was Mrs. Thorton hurrying away. Kurt the reporter was following her.

"Hey!" George exclaimed. "Let's follow them!"

Nancy shook her head. "You can't follow them if they aren't moving," she pointed out. "Look!"

Mrs. Thorton was now standing very still watching everyone in the contest. Her mouth was turned down. "Why does she look so unhappy?" Nancy asked.

"Maybe because of what happened in the contest," Lisa said.

"I know just how she feels," Nancy said, sitting on the sand. She looked at the way the castle had been smashed in and she felt awful inside. She looked at the green sand and she felt mad. Then she looked at the STAY AWAY written in the sand. She took a finger and in a clean patch of sand wrote her own STAY AWAY.

Nancy's eyes lit up. "Wait a minute!" she said. "I've got it!"

"Got what?" Bess asked excitedly. "Do you know who wrecked our castle?"

"No," admitted Nancy, "but I have an idea. Look at this!" Nancy pointed to the letters. "See how they slant to the left?"

"Yes, so what?" Lisa asked.

"I'm right-handed and the letters I wrote slant to the right! So whoever wrote this first one must be left-handed!"

Caught Left-handed!

Nancy took out her notebook and found the page that said "Clues." "Suspect is left-handed," she wrote.

"But which suspect?" Lisa asked

"Girls! Who would like some lunch?" Hannah Gruen called. Nancy looked up. Hannah was on the porch of their cottage.

Nancy looked around the beach. Just about everyone else, it seemed, was leaving for lunch, too. "Do you want to come for lunch?" Nancy asked Lisa.

Lisa stood up. "Sure, thanks. I just have to tell my dad," she said quickly. "He's over there on the beach."

"I can't eat anything," Bess said, standing up. "I'm too upset."

"That will be a first, then!" Nancy laughed, trying to cheer up Bess.

The inside of the cottage smelled delicious. Nancy's father was already at the table. "Macaroni and cheese," he said. "Come sit down."

The girls waited quietly until there was a knock on the door. "Hi, I'm Lisa," Lisa said to Hannah and Mr. Drew.

"Any friend of the girls is a friend of mine," Mr. Drew said. "Please sit down and eat."

Lisa was out of breath. "I ran all the way," she said.

The girls began eating quickly. "I can't wait to get back to the beach," Nancy said. "I just have to figure this case out."

"Finish your lunch first," said Nancy's father. "Remember, you can't solve mysteries on an empty stomach."

When the girls were finished eating, Nancy started to clear the plates. "Oh, don't bother," Hannah said. "I know you girls are anxious to get back to the beach."

"Thank you, Hannah!" said Nancy. The girls ran back down to the beach.

"Oh no!" George cried. "Look!"

Nancy looked down, shocked. The STAY AWAY had been erased!

"Who did this? And why? And how did they do it without anyone seeing them?" Nancy cried. She looked around at the other teams. "Lara! Jane!" Nancy called. Lara and Jane looked up. "Did you see anyone around our castle when we weren't here?"

"I wasn't really paying attention," Jane said. "Why? What happened?"

"The 'stay away' in the sand is gone," George said.

Jane frowned. "Well, don't look at us. We didn't do it!"

"No one said you did," Bess told them.

Lisa bent down. "This is terrible," she said. "Now we'll never find out who wrote it."

"Oh, yes we will," Nancy said. "Or I'm not Nancy Drew the detective!"

"Look," George said, staring straight ahead. "Maybe this is a new clue."

Ahead of them Kurt the reporter was

talking to Mrs. Thorton. He was writing something. "*He's* using his left hand!" Nancy said.

Kurt suddenly turned and looked right at the girls, almost as if he knew they were talking about him. "Look how guilty he looks," George said.

"Looking guilty isn't the same as being guilty," Nancy said. "Let's go over and talk to him."

The girls walked over. Mrs. Thorton suddenly stopped talking. "Did you need something, girls?" said Mrs. Thorton. Her voice sounded funny to Nancy, as if she had been crying.

"Is something wrong?" asked Kurt, his eyes bright.

"The 'stay away' sign is gone!" George blurted.

"What?" gasped Mrs. Thorton.

"But we still have a clue," Nancy continued. "We figured out that someone who is left-handed must have written it." She looked at Kurt's left hand.

"Wait a minute," Kurt said. "Why are you looking at me like that? Hold on. You don't think that I wrote that 'stay away' in the sand because I'm left-handed do you? Why would I do that?"

"You told us trouble sells newspapers," Nancy said.

"I write about trouble. I don't make it!" Kurt exclaimed.

"But you looked so upset," Nancy said.

"I'll tell you why he's so upset," Mrs. Thorton said. "Kurt's interviewing me for the newspaper." Mrs. Thorton lowered her eyes. "I wasn't going to tell anyone yet, but I'm thinking about retiring. Kurt's trying to talk me out of it."

"She can't retire!" Kurt said. "Without her, there really wouldn't be a contest. She organizes the judges, the prizes, the whole ceremony."

"I don't want my last contest to be one with trouble," said Mrs. Thorton sadly.

Nancy bit her lip. "Then it's even more important than ever for us to solve this mystery."

"You come up with anything, you let me know," Kurt said. "I'll make it front page news. And that's a promise."

Nancy pulled out her notebook and crossed off the word "reporter" on her suspect list. Then the girls went back to the sand castle and got to work. Nancy began making a patio out of tiny stones. Bess sprinkled the new glittery sand on the roof of the castle, and George went to get water to pack the sand down more.

"Who would do such a thing?" Nancy said out loud. She often did her best thinking that way.

"I'd better go check in with my dad," Lisa said. "I promised I'd come see him when we got back from lunch."

"See you later, alligator," said Bess.

"In a while, crocodile," said George.

"It will be a thriller, gorilla," Lisa called, laughing.

Shortly after Lisa left, Katharine came by. She was wearing a bright yellow swimsuit and carrying a beach towel.

"Here comes Miss Friendly," said Bess.

"Come on, that's not nice," Nancy said. "Give her a chance."

"Hi," Katharine said, and Nancy smiled.

"Hi back to you," said George.

Katharine suddenly dug into her beach bag and brought out a comb. "Want to borrow this? You can make cool patterns by raking it across the sand," she said.

"Sure!" Bess said. "Are you in the contest, too?"

Katharine shrugged. "Oh, not this year," she said. She handed the comb to Bess.

"Oh, let me try!" said George.

"I'll just go get some more water," Nancy said.

Nancy ran to the water, swinging the pail. Lara and Jane were already there, filling their pails. "Hey," Jane said. "How come you have so much extra help? First Lisa, and now Katharine."

"I think it's nice they're helping," Nancy said.

"Well, neither one of them would be helping if they could enter the contest themselves," Lara said.

Nancy stood up. She knew Lisa couldn't enter because she had already won, but she didn't know why Katharine couldn't. "Why can't Katharine enter?" Nancy said.

"Duh—Earth to Nancy," said Jane meanly.

"Because Katharine's mother owns Peppermint Park, and Peppermint Park gives out the winning prizes. It wouldn't be fair if Katharine could enter. If she won, everyone would think the contest was fixed. That's why this time of year Katharine's always in a bad mood."

Nancy was shocked. Maybe that was why Katharine hadn't been nice to them at first. Katharine probably felt jealous. But why was Katharine being nice to them now?

Nancy walked back toward the castle. Sometimes, she thought, the only way to get at the truth was to ask for it.

Nancy walked swiftly back to the beach. All the girls were patting the edges of the castle. Nancy stared at Katharine. Katharine was making a whirling pattern in the sand, and she was doing it with her left hand!

"Katharine," said Nancy, "are you left-handed?"

Katharine put her hand down. "So what?" she asked.

"The person who wrote 'stay away' was left-handed," Nancy said.

"Katharine, you didn't!" Bess cried.

Katharine stood up. Her face grew very red. "Just because I'm left-handed doesn't mean I did something like that!" Katharine cried. She looked over at the beach where Lisa was running toward them. "But I know who did! I didn't want to say anything, in case I was wrong about this, but one night, when I was running to Peppermint Park to help, I saw only one person on the beach."

"Who?" Nancy asked.

"I'll tell you only if you don't tell her I told you," Katharine said. "I don't want anyone mad at me. And I'm not going to go over there with you to accuse her."

"Agreed," Nancy said.

"Agreed," repeated Bess and George.

Katharine pointed to Lisa, who was down the beach near her father. "There she is! There's the person who wrecked your castle! It's Lisa!"

6

Un-buried Treasure

"Lisa!" Nancy exclaimed. She couldn't believe it.

"Remember when Lisa ran to tell her dad she was meeting us for lunch?" George said. "When we all went back to the beach, the 'stay away' was gone! Lisa must have erased it then."

Nancy shook her head. "I still can't believe it," she said. But there was only one way to find out if it was true, and that was to go and talk to Lisa. The girls ran across the sand to Lisa.

"Lisa, did you wreck our castle?" Bess demanded.

Lisa's mouth dropped open. "Is this a joke?" she demanded.

Nancy shook her head. "Someone told us they saw you on the beach that night."

"Someone! Someone who?" Lisa asked.

"I can't tell you that. But can you tell us if that's true?" Nancy asked.

"Yes, it's true," Lisa said, "but not for the reason you think!"

Lisa pointed to the other side of the beach. "See that man in the blue bathing suit?" Lisa asked. "That's my father. He'll prove I didn't do it!"

The girls silently walked over to Lisa's father. "Dad?" Lisa said. Lisa's father sat up, smiling.

"I was just thinking I would walk over and check on you," he said. He looked at the other girls. "Are these the new friends you were telling your mother and me about?" he said. "I'm so happy to meet all of you, girls. I'm so sorry, too, about what happened to your sand castle, but I know you will rebuild it better than ever.

"What's the matter?" Lisa's father asked. "You all look as if the ocean had dried up!"

"Someone blamed me for wrecking the sand castle!" Lisa said. "Just because they saw me on the beach that night! Will you tell them where I was—and why?"

Lisa's father frowned.

"Dad, remember yesterday when you came to take me to the dentist?" Lisa asked. "You didn't want to get your good shoes wet so you stood at the edge of the beach waiting for me?"

"Yes, I remember," he said. He looked at the other girls. "When Lisa came off the beach she pointed out the castle to me. I remember thinking how great it looked."

"The castle was still there?" Nancy asked.

"Certainly it was," Lisa's father said. "Number nine. And Lisa was with me for the rest of the time. We went to the dentist and then back home and I took her back to the beach this morning myself. She couldn't have had time to destroy your castle."

Nancy frowned. "Lisa, we're sorry we accused you, but if you didn't destroy our castle, then who did?"

"I don't know," Lisa said.

"But I bet you girls will find out," her father said kindly.

The four girls walked back to the castle. No one felt like working. The sun beat down on them, and the girls began to get really hot.

Just then Mr. Drew came out onto the beach, carrying a towel. "Why don't you girls take a break and take a swim?" he asked.

"We can't!" Nancy wailed. "We don't have enough clues yet."

"Take a break and you'll think clearer," Mr. Drew said. "I'll watch you from right over there." He pointed to a patch of sand.

George scanned the horizon. "We could swim out to the kiddie float," she said, pointing to the big yellow raft.

"All right," Nancy said. "But let's not just swim, let's race!"

The girls ran into the water. The waves lapped at their legs and the water was so cool and delicious Nancy felt as if she could have stayed in it forever. Nancy got to the raft first.

Dripping water, she tugged herself up on the raft. Her eyes opened wide. Katharine was lying on the raft, and she was crying.

"Katharine," Nancy said, and Katharine looked up. Her eyes were red and her face was tear-streaked. Bess, George, and Lisa pulled themselves up on the raft, too. "What's wrong?" Nancy asked.

"I've had a bad day," Katharine said, sitting up. She pushed her long braids behind her shoulders.

"You think *you've* had a bad day!" Lisa said. "You should hear about mine! Someone thought *I* destroyed the sand castle! Can you believe it? Of course I didn't do it!"

Katharine sat up. "Do you have any new suspects?" she asked Nancy.

"No," Nancy said slowly.

"But we'll find one," Bess said. "No one is a better detective than Nancy Drew."

Katharine moved to the edge of the raft with a start. "Last one to shore is a piece of seaweed!" she called, and dove right into the water.

"Hey, I'm no seaweed!" shouted George, jumping in after her. Bess jumped in, and then Lisa, with Nancy leaping after her.

Katharine was really fast. She was on

shore before any of the girls. "I won! I won!" Katharine cried happily, clapping her hands.

Bess plucked up a pretty shell and handed it to Katharine. "And here's your trophy." She laughed. Katharine ran her fingers over the shell. "I've never had a trophy before!" she said excitedly.

"Wait! Let's take the winner's picture," Nancy said. "My camera is right in my beach bag."

The girls ran to their bags, pulling out their cameras. Katharine posed with her shell. "The winner!" Nancy said. "The last shot," Nancy said. "My film is finished."

"Mine was finished this morning," George said.

Bess grabbed for her camera. "All of you stand together," she urged. "I have one picture left!"

The four girls linked arms and smiled. "Say sand castle!" Bess said.

"Sand castle!" called the girls and Bess snapped.

"I'd better get back home," Katharine said.

"And we'd better get back to work," Bess

said. "Maybe while we build, we'll find some more clues."

The girls worked hard on the castle. George took a small melon scoop Hannah had loaned them and dug a moat. "This is going to be the best moat ever," George said, and then she suddenly stopped digging.

"What is it?" Nancy asked.

"Buried treasure," George said, lifting up something sparkling and shiny. It was a small, glittery red stone. But whose was it? And what was it doing in their castle?

7

A Clue in the Picture

"I don't know what this means," Nancy said. "but it means something." She carefully took the stone and put it into her beach bag. "Let's keep working."

Nancy took her pail down to the edge of the water and filled it. George collected the prettiest stones she could find to add to the little patio Nancy had started building in the back of the castle. Bess and Lisa were busy using a plastic paper clip to press in designs along the base of the castle.

By the time Mr. Drew came by to collect the girls to go home, Nancy's nose was sunburned, George's fingernails were caked with sand, and Bess and Lisa had built an entire moat around the castle.

"I'll see you tomorrow," Lisa said, waving.

"We're finished," Nancy told her father. "And so is the film in our cameras."

"Fantastic!" Mr. Drew said.

"Tomorrow afternoon is the contest judging," Bess said. "I think we have a chance of winning!"

"You girls have worked so hard, we should celebrate tonight," Mr. Drew said.

"Celebrate how?" Nancy asked.

Mr. Drew's eyes sparkled. "Who here likes pizza and miniature golf?" he asked. "There's a pizza parlor and a miniature golf course on the same street as the one-hour photo store. We can drop off your pictures, play golf, and by the time we're hungry for pizza, the pictures will be ready."

The girls jumped up and down. "I think tonight is going to be great," Nancy said.

That evening, Mr. Drew drove the girls to the one-hour photo shop and then they walked next door to Pirate's Cove Miniature Golf. The entrance was a huge pirate with an eye patch, standing with his legs far apart.

"Come on, let's play!" Nancy cried.

There were a lot of people playing, and the girls had to sit on a bench and wait. Finally, it was their turn. "You go first," Nancy said to Bess.

The first hole was a straight path to a big fish. They had to hit the ball into the fish's mouth. Bess swung and the ball bounced along, missing the hole. "Oh well, it's still fun," Bess said. "Even if I don't get the best score."

Nancy took her shot, moving her club carefully. Her ball missed the hole, too. Laughing, she stepped aside so her father could play. "Your turn, Dad," she said.

"Hey, isn't that Katharine's mother over there?" Bess said. Nancy looked up and saw Katharine's mother playing golf with another woman. "Hi, Mrs. Rhodes," Nancy called.

Mrs. Rhodes looked up. For a minute, she didn't seem to know them.

"We're Nancy, Bess, and George," Nancy said. "We met Katharine today at Peppermint Park. And this is my dad."

"Hello," said Mr. Drew.

Mrs. Rhodes smiled and shook Mr. Drew's hand. Then she smiled back at the girls. "Oh, of course," said Mrs. Rhodes. "You're the girls who had that awful problem with your sand castle."

"Gee, I guess we don't need Kurt to spread the news. Everyone already knows it," George said.

"Where's Katharine?" Nancy said, looking around. "We'd love to play golf with her."

"She's at home searching for something she lost," said Mrs. Rhodes. "She was determined to keep looking."

"She lost something?" Nancy asked.

"She won't even tell me what it is," Mrs. Rhodes said. "Though if she did, I could help her look for it."

"That's probably why she was crying today," Bess said. "When I lost my favorite necklace, I cried for weeks until I found it."

"I'll tell her you said hello," said Mrs. Rhodes. "Oh, it's my turn now," she said. "You have a good time."

The girls and Mr. Drew went back to

their game. The course was so much fun! One hole had a giant octopus on it, another had a big anchor, and Nancy's favorite was one with a mermaid with a shiny green tail! By the time they finished, Bess had the highest score, and then George. Mr. Drew and Nancy were tied. "Oh well, we might not be champion miniature golfers, but we sure know how to have fun!" Nancy said.

"That's right, Pudding Pie," said Mr. Drew ruffling her hair. "Let's go get the pictures now, and then have some pizza."

They quickly went into the one-hour photo store to pick up the pictures. "I can't wait to see them!" Nancy said.

"I can't wait to eat pizza!" George exclaimed.

Mr. Drew laughed. "Well, you girls can do both. Come on, let's go eat."

The Leaning Tower of Pizza had long wooden tables and bright red-checked tablecloths. There were ten different kinds of pizza toppings.

"I want green peppers!" Nancy said excitedly.

"Mushrooms!" said Bess.

"Pineapple!" George cried.

"Ew! Pineapple! Are you sure?" Bess said, making a face.

"Well, I thought I'd try something new," George said.

"How about if we order one big pizza with everything on it?" suggested Mr. Drew.

"That sounds positively yummy," said George.

While they were waiting for the pizza, the girls looked at their pictures. There were shots of them all standing together. There was a great shot of Nancy with Lisa and Katharine. And there were many shots of all the different castles.

"Your castle looks terrific," said Mr. Drew.

"I hope it stays that way," Nancy said glumly. "But if we don't find out who destroyed it, they might do it again. And tomorrow afternoon is the judging! We don't have much time."

Nancy studied a picture of Katharine she had taken the first day they had met her in Peppermint Park. Then, she suddenly noticed something. A clue!

"It's as plain as the nose on my face!" Nancy exclaimed.

"What is?" said Bess.

Nancy pointed to the picture. "Look," she said. "Look at Katharine in this picture."

"Yeah, so?" said Bess. "I'm looking but I'm not seeing what you're seeing."

Nancy pointed to Katharine's hand. "The ring!" Nancy said. "The stone is bright and shiny, and it's red—like the stone we found in the castle!"

"You think that stone was Katharine's?" said George.

"I think I can prove it was!" Nancy exclaimed. She carefully tucked the picture into her beach bag. "Tomorrow, we'll find out," Nancy said. "And I know just how to do it!"

The next morning was Monday, the day of the judging, and the girls asked for permission to go to Peppermint Park. "Ice cream in the morning?" Hannah frowned.

"Not ice cream," Nancy said. "Proof. I think I know who ruined our castle."

"Well, then, that's different," Hannah

said. "Since it's so close, you can go."

The girls hurried to Peppermint Park. As soon as they got there, Nancy went right over to Katharine. Nancy looked quickly at Katharine's hands. She was wearing red rings on both hands, and for a moment, Nancy wondered if she had made a mistake.

Nancy took the stone out of her purse and showed it to Katharine. Instantly, Katharine's face lit up. "You found the stone from my favorite ring!" she exclaimed happily. "I've been looking all over for it! I thought I lost it. I was so upset I couldn't even tell anyone."

"You did lose it," Nancy told her. "In our sand castle."

Katharine's face turned as red as the stone in her ring.

"I think you destroyed our castle," Nancy said. "And I think I know why!"

8

It Wasn't on Purpose!

It wasn't on purpose!" Katharine said. "I can explain."

"You really did destroy our castle?" Bess said, astonished. "But why?"

Katharine hung her head. "It was an accident!"

"Writing 'stay away' was an accident?" Bess asked.

"No," Katharine said in a small voice. "That part wasn't."

"What happened?" Nancy asked.

"I was running to the shop to help my mother and I was late, so I took a short cut across the beach," Katharine said. "Only a few people were there and I saw Lisa running across the sand."

"You really did see Lisa?" Nancy asked.

Katharine nodded. "Then Lisa's father showed up and called to her. After Lisa was gone, I walked over to the sand castles. I just wanted to look at them. I started thinking about what a wonderful castle I could build if I had a chance. I thought it was unfair that you were from out of town and you got to enter the contest and I didn't. And the more I thought about it, the madder I got! So I wrote 'stay away.' I thought that it would scare you and then maybe you wouldn't want to be in the contest anymore." She hung her head unhappily. "But then *I* got scared that someone would catch me so I started to run away and tripped—right into the castle!"

"That's not being our friend!" George said.

"I know!" Katharine cried. "And I felt so bad about it that I couldn't think about anything else! So the next day, I came back at lunchtime when no one was really around to erase what I had written. I even tried to rebuild the castle a little, but I made it even more of a mess so I just ran away. That must have been when I lost the stone in my ring."

"Why didn't you tell us?" Bess asked.

Katharine shook her head. "I didn't think you'd ever be able to forgive me. The only way I could think to make it up to you was to help you with the castle. I guess I ruined that, too."

"But you blamed Lisa!" Bess exclaimed. "You made us think she might have done it!"

Katharine started to cry. "When you asked me if I did it, I got so scared. I didn't know what to do or what to say. I was so afraid to tell you the truth so I blurted out Lisa's name. I feel so bad that I ruined your castle and that I didn't tell you the truth. I'm sorry. Will you ever be my friends again?"

The girls were quiet. Then Nancy sighed. "Friends make mistakes," she said. "And you felt bad for what you did and tried to make it up to us. And you apologized. Of course we'll be your friends."

"I want to apologize to Lisa and Mrs. Thorton, too," Katharine said.

"Maybe you should start by forgiving yourself a little," a voice said.

The girls all turned. There was Mrs. Rhodes, standing there, her arms folded.

"Mom!" said Katharine. "I can explain!"

Mrs. Rhodes shook her head. "What you did may have been an accident, Katharine, but not telling the truth about it at first wasn't right. I'm glad that you are apologizing."

"I'll do anything to make things right," Katharine said.

"What else do you think you should do?" Mrs. Rhodes gently asked.

Katharine was quiet for a moment and then her face lit up. "I know!" she said. "I've been saving these glittery Popsicle sticks. I was going to make my own castle out of them." Katharine turned to the girls. "I want you to have them."

"Are you sure?" Nancy asked.

"I've never been more sure," said Katharine. "I have them in the back of the store."

Katharine ran to the back and returned with her hands full of the most beautiful Popsicle sticks Nancy had ever seen. They were sparkled with red and blue swirls.

"Oh, thank you!" Nancy cried.

"That's a very nice thing you just did, Katharine," said Mrs. Rhodes. "I've been thinking, though. Maybe what I've been doing isn't right, either. Maybe next year, you can enter the contest."

"But how can I do that?" Katharine said. "Peppermint Park gives out the prize. It won't be fair if I enter."

"Well, maybe Peppermint Park is due for a break," said Mrs. Rhodes. "Maybe the Leaning Tower of Pizza can offer all the pizza you can eat."

Katharine smiled. "Really? You'd really do that?"

Katharine's mother put her arm about her daughter. "I'd really do that."

"I'm going to go find Lisa and Mrs. Thorton now," said Katharine.

Nancy held up the beautiful Popsicle sticks. "And we really have to go to work," she said. "The judging is this afternoon."

* * *

The girls quickly finished putting up the Popsicle stick fence around their castle and then went home to change into sundresses. Mr. Drew and Hannah walked with the girls to the beach.

"Oh, look!" exclaimed Nancy. "They put up a little stage."

"And rows of seats," added George.

In front of all the sand castles was a small wooden platform. On top of the platform was a table with three shiny trophies that looked like golden sand shovels. There were three chairs and three people sitting in the chairs. "Those must be the judges," said Mr. Drew.

"Let's sit right up front," Nancy said. "So we can see what's going on. Maybe we can tell who the judges will choose just by the expressions on their faces."

"You're always looking for clues!" Mr. Drew laughed, ruffling Nancy's hair.

They all sat down. Soon almost all the seats were filled. Everyone was so excited, Nancy could feel it in the air.

Mrs. Thorton stepped onto the stage. She

was all dressed up in a short-sleeved dress with a big red flower on the collar. Beside her was Kurt Jeffers. "I hope Katharine and Lisa made up," Bess said. She looked around. "I don't see either one of them anywhere."

"Let's save them a seat," Bess said.

Nancy looked around, too. She had never felt more nervous. Would they win?

"There go the judges," Mr. Drew said. He pointed to three adults who were walking around the castles.

"Oh, I hope, I hope we win!" Bess moaned.

"There's James," Bess said, pointing to James who was holding a young girl's hand. The little girl had hair as red as James's. "That must be the little sister he was making the green sandbox for."

"And there's Katharine and Lisa," Nancy said. She waved and the two girls came over.

"Mrs. Thorton was great!" Katharine exclaimed. "She said that my feeling bad was punishment enough. She's not going to tell anyone!"

"Tell anyone what?" said Kurt Jeffers,

suddenly appearing. "Is there a story somewhere that I need to hear?"

"Not that we know of," said Nancy quickly.

"It doesn't matter, because I have a real scoop!" said Kurt.

"You do?" Nancy said. She hoped he wasn't going to say he was writing a story about Katharine causing all the trouble. She had apologized and that was enough for Nancy.

"Mrs. Thorton isn't going to retire after all!" Kurt exclaimed. "She said that having everything turn out all right made her realize how much she loved this contest."

"The judging will now begin!" called Mrs. Thorton.

Everyone stood along the beach watching the judges. They seemed to take forever. They stood in front of each castle. They crouched down and frowned. When the judges got to Nancy, Bess, and George's castle, Nancy held her breath. Her father rubbed her shoulders. "Pudding Pie, your castle is wonderful," he whispered. "And no matter whether you get a prize or not, as far as I'm concerned, you've won!"

Nancy looked over and saw Lara and Jane, in summer dresses, sitting way in the back. They looked really nervous, too.

The judges walked over to Mrs. Thorton and whispered something to her. She smiled and nodded. "We have our winners!" she announced.

Nancy held her father's hand tightly.

"First prize—castle number eight! Lara and Jane!"

Nancy clapped hard.

"Their castle is great," Bess admitted.

"Second prize—" said Mrs. Thorton. "Number nine! Nancy, Bess, and George!"

Nancy jumped up and down. Bess clapped her hands and hugged George. "We won second prize!" said Nancy.

"Hooray! Hooray!" cried Katharine.

"Yay!" shouted Lisa.

"Great work, girls!" said Mr. Drew.

"Third prize," said Mrs. Thorton. "Number one! Ronald Tiger!" A small boy started cheering.

"Will the winners come forward and get their pictures taken?" said Mrs. Thorton.

"Will we ever!" said Bess. The girls walked

forward and stood in a line on a small platform. Mrs. Thorton had one small gold trophy in the shape of a sand shovel. Printed on it was SECOND PRIZE ECHO LAKE SAND CASTLE CONTEST.

"Who gets it?" Bess whispered to Nancy.

"We'll *all* share," Nancy said firmly. "We can keep it one week at your house, one week at George's, and then it's my turn."

"Say cheese!" cried Kurt Jeffers as he snapped pictures of the girls.

"Wait," said Nancy to Kurt. "Can Lisa and Katharine get their pictures taken with us, too? They helped us so much. We couldn't have done it without them!"

Katharine and Lisa smiled.

"Sure, why not?" Kurt said.

"Wait until we get home," said George. "Brenda is going to be so jealous when she sees our pictures in the paper. Let's bring an issue home."

"No," said Nancy. "Let's bring an issue home so we can share it. Being jealous does nothing but cause trouble."

Mr. Drew approached. "Let's all go out for ice cream," he said.

SANDCASTLE BUILDING
CONTEST

* * *

That night in the cottage, Nancy took out her notebook and wrote:

The sand castle case is over. And so is our vacation here. But I've learned one thing.

She crossed that out.

But I've learned TWO things from this case. One. It's better to share than to be jealous about what you don't have. And two. Sometimes you have to dig deep for clues. But the real buried treasure is in friendship!

Case closed.

THIRD-GRADE DETECTIVES

Everyone in the third-grade loves the new teacher, Mr. Merlin.
Mr. Merlin used to be a spy, and he knows all about secret codes and the strange and gross ways the police solve mysteries.

YOU CAN HELP DECODE THE CLUES AND SOLVE THE MYSTERY IN THESE OTHER STORIES ABOUT THE THIRD-GRADE DETECTIVES:

#1 The Clue of the Left-handed Envelope

#2 The Puzzle of the Pretty Pink Handkerchief

#3 The Mystery of the Hairy Tomatoes

#4 The Cobweb Confession

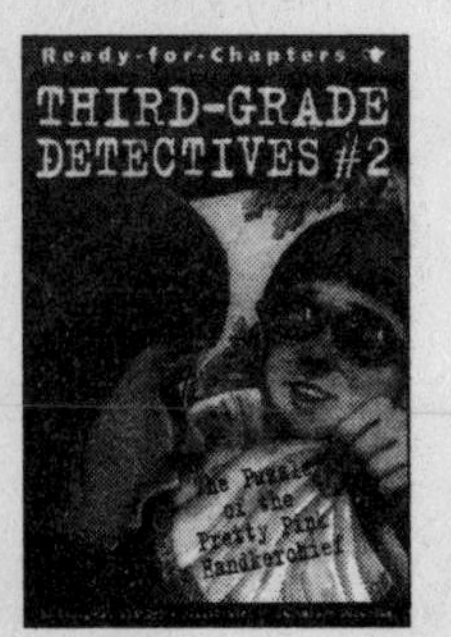

ALADDIN PAPERBACKS
Simon & Schuster Children's Publishing • www.SimonSaysKids.com

Ready-for-Chapters